The Hickory Chair

by LISA ROWE
FRAUSTINO

illustrated by
BENNY
ANDREWS

SCHOLASTIC INC.

New York Toronto London Auckland Sydney
Mexico City New Delhi Hong Kong Buenos Aires

Text copyright © 2001 by Lisa Rowe Fraustino. Illustrations copyright © 2001 by Benny Andrews. All rights reserved. Published by Scholastic Inc. SCHOLASTIC, SCHOLASTIC PRESS, the LANTERN LOGO and associated logos are trademarks and/or registered trademarks of Scholastic Inc.

Arthur A. Levine Books hardcover edition published by Arthur A. Levine Books, an imprint of Scholastic Press, February 2001

ISBN 0-590-52252-3

12 11 10 9   7 8 9/0

Printed in the U.S.A.   08

First Scholastic paperback printing, February 2004

The text type is set in 17-point Goudy Modern MT. Display type is set in Steam. • The artwork is done in oils and fabric collage. • Book design by Marijka Kostiw.

WE WOULD LIKE TO THANK OUR COLLEAGUES AT THE NATIONAL BRAILLE PRESS FOR THEIR HELP AND ADVICE ON THIS BOOK.

For Olivia, in memory of her godfather,
Louis D. Mitchell
— L. R. F.

To my grandson,
Casey Robert Andrews
— B. A.

Sundays when I was small, that Gran of mine was good at hiding. The first time I played hide-and-seek with her and the older grandchildren, she disguised me as the pillow on the bed that Gramps had carved long ago for my father. Nobody found me.

When I was the seeker, I could almost always sniff everyone out,

even Gran the time she stood inside her robe behind the bathroom

door. She had a good alive smell—lilacs, with a whiff of bleach.

I loved Gran's smell, and her warm face when we played touch-your-nose at the gold mirror, and her salty kisses when we sat on Gramps's old army trunk in the attic and listened to the wind sing on the roof.

Most of all, I loved her molasses voice as she read to me out loud.

"You're my favorite youngest grandchild, Louis, and this is my favorite chair," she'd tell me. "Gramps carved it from a hickory that once grew on this very spot." She clapped her hands together. Lilac and bleach danced around.

"Every time I sit in this chair, I lean back, shut my eyes, and see that old hickory tickling the belly of the sun."

"Me too," I said, and I really did see it, even though I was born blind.

"You got blind sight," said Gran, and she tickled my nose.

So the Sundays went until one day in school, I felt my father's shadow cold on my cheek. He told me Gran had died.

At the funeral I touched her hand to say good-bye. It was cold and smelled too much of lilacs, not enough of bleach.

Afterwards the family went to Gran's house to hear her will. Around her rocker it was hard to breathe. I sat on my father's lap.

When every eye had been cried dry, Uncle Lofton blew his nose one last time and said, "Remember how Gran used to surprise us with notes hidden under pillows, between book pages, in pockets, and anywhere else she could connive?"

My father laughed. "Once she sneaked into Gramps's workplace and left him a love note—in the wrong lunch box!"

"Remember," I began, "when I was a baby and Gran was rocking me to sleep in her favorite chair, but when she stood up to take me to the crib, the chair came with me?"

My mother picked up the story. "You'd poked this hole right here,"—her fingernail scratched wood—"and made a ball of batting in your little fist!"

"Well," sighed Aunt Candy-May, "let's see what's to become of that chair now."

Her purse clicked open; I knew what it was because leather and peppermint smells jumped right out. Paper crackled like hickory limbs in the wind, and Aunt Candy-May commenced to read Gran's will. It didn't take long. "To each of my favorite people I leave a note hidden in one of my favorite things. Keep those things. Sell whatever's left and split the money between Candy-May, Lofton, and Louis Senior."

"That rascal Gran," my father said fondly.

Smells swirled with excitement as we all dashed off to search Gran's favorite things.

As the others peered into nooks and crannies, I felt the mirror slowly, inch by inch, until I pinched a bud of paper under a gold leaf.

Hoping it was my note, I rushed to Aunt Candy-May.

She read, "For my favorite middlest grandchild." That was Cousin Lucille.

After that, the grandchildren raced to the attic and searched the army trunk where we and Gran had listened to the wind sing. Stowed beneath the canvas lining I found a note. "For my favorite grandson born on Tuesday." Cousin Bill-Bob.

I found a slip of paper holding a place in the tattered Bible where Gran had recorded her family stories. "For my favorite tallest son." My father.

Believe it or not, nobody else had found any notes yet. I told you

that Gran of mine was good at hiding!

"Louis, did Gran tell you where to look?" my brother asked.

"No, but she said I got blind sight," I answered.

"If that's what it is, I'm closing my eyes." My brother hurried off

to use blind sight on the bed Gramps had carved for our father,

where Gran had hidden me the first time I played hide-and-seek.

Remembering that, I hoped Gran had left my note there.

But the note my brother coaxed from behind a knot in the head-
board said, "For my favorite eldest grandson whose father
snored here." My brother.

Now it seemed that the entire
family had got blind
sight.

Before long, they all had their notes. All except for me. I was a finder but not a keeper.

"How could Gran forget her favorite youngest grandchild?" I cried.

"She couldn't," said my father. "Mark my words, that note will turn up."

We searched everywhere—even Gran's sewing machine, her bronze lamps with fringed shades, her kitchen table with six rickety chairs. But there was only one thing left that I thought Gran would want me to have. Gramps had carved it from a hickory that tickled the sun. The air around it was hard to breathe.

I held my breath and felt Gran's favorite chair inch by inch, carefully, as if it were made of dried leaves. I dug up a nickel, the cap of a pen, a hairpin, a button, and—at last—a scrid of paper! The air suddenly tasted light and sweet.

Aunt Candy-May read, "Baking soda, salt, bleach. . . . Oh, Louis, we're so sorry!"

"Louis is the youngest," said my brother. "Could Gran have left the notes before he was born and then forgotten to add his?"

Silence sucked everyone's breath away, and the air curdled in my throat. I ran out of Gran's house.

Many Sundays we searched for the note over and over, to no avail, until it came time to sell the rest of Gran's things.

"Just pick out something you want, Louis," said my father. "Anything at all."

Carefully I climbed onto Gran's favorite chair and leaned back. The cushion sighed a good clean smell, lilacs, with a whiff of bleach. Gran's shape was rocked into the seat. As I jiggled to fit, I heard her molasses voice pour out, "You're my favorite youngest grandchild, Louis. . . ."

The lost note no longer mattered. In that chair, I was on Gran's lap again.

Now I am as old as Gran when she hid her messages. Not so long ago, when I thought my favorite youngest grandchild was asleep, she poked her hand in this hole right here and made a ball of batting in her little fist. When I unfolded her fingers I found a wad of paper. And I swear it smelled of lilacs and a whiff of bleach.

"For my favorite youngest grandchild with blind sight."